TRACKING THE GIGANTIC BEAST

DINOSAUR COVE™

TRACKING THE GIGANTIC BEAST

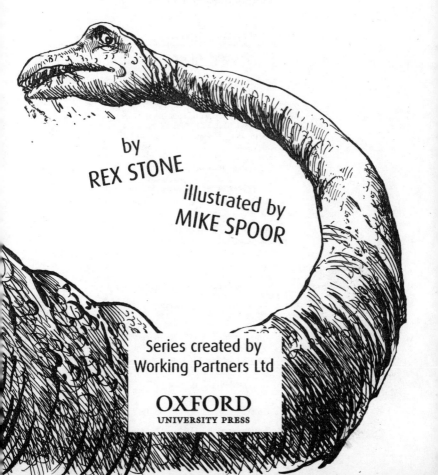

by
REX STONE

illustrated by
MIKE SPOOR

Series created by
Working Partners Ltd

OXFORD
UNIVERSITY PRESS

For Andy and Rob, with love - R.S
For my Hannah, at last - M.S

OXFORD
UNIVERSITY PRESS

Great Clarendon Street, Oxford OX2 6DP
Oxford University Press is a department of the University of Oxford.
It furthers the University's objective of excellence in research, scholarship,
and education by publishing worldwide in

Oxford   New York

Auckland   Cape Town   Dar es Salaam   Hong Kong   Karachi
Kuala Lumpur   Madrid   Melbourne   Mexico City   Nairobi
New Delhi   Shanghai   Taipei   Toronto

With offices in

Argentina   Austria   Brazil   Chile   Czech Republic   France   Greece
Guatemala   Hungary   Italy   Japan   Poland   Portugal   Singapore
South Korea   Switzerland   Thailand   Turkey   Ukraine   Vietnam

Oxford is a registered trade mark of Oxford University Press
in the UK and in certain other countries

© Working Partners Limited 2009
Illustrations © Mike Spoor 2009
Eye logo © Dominic Harman 2009

Series created by Working Partners Ltd

Dinosaur Cove is a registered trademark or Working Partners Ltd

The moral rights of the author have been asserted

Database right Oxford University Press (maker)

First published 2009

British Library Cataloguing in Publication Data

Data available

ISBN: 978-0-19-272894-4

1 3 5 7 9 10 8 6 4 2

Printed in Great Britain by CPI Cox and Wyman, Reading, Berkshire
Paper used in the production of this book is a natural,
recyclable product made from wood grown in sustainable forests
The manufacturing process conforms to the environmental
regulations of the country of origin

FACT FILE

➡️ JAMIE AND HIS BEST FRIEND, TOM, HAVE DISCOVERED A SECRET CAVE WITH FOSSILIZED DINOSAUR FOOTPRINTS AND, WHEN THEY PLACE THEIR FEET OVER EACH OF THE FOSSILS IN TURN, THEY ARE MAGICALLY TRANSPORTED TO A WORLD WITH REAL, LIVE DINOSAURS. BUT THE BOYS NEVER IMAGINED THAT VISITING DINO WORLD WOULD BE JUST LIKE GOING TO THE DENTIST...

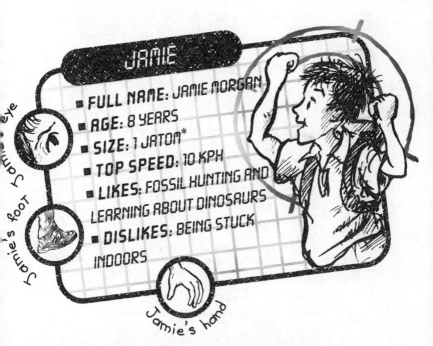

JAMIE

- **FULL NAME:** JAMIE MORGAN
- **AGE:** 8 YEARS
- **SIZE:** 1 JATOM*
- **TOP SPEED:** 10 KPH
- **LIKES:** FOSSIL HUNTING AND LEARNING ABOUT DINOSAURS
- **DISLIKES:** BEING STUCK INDOORS

Jamie's eye

Jamie's foot

Jamie's hand

*NOTE: A JATOM IS THE SIZE OF JAMIE OR TOM: 125 CM TALL AND 27 KG IN WEIGHT

TOM

- **FULL NAME:** THOMAS CLAY
- **AGE:** 8 YEARS
- **SIZE:** 1 JATOM*
- **TOP SPEED:** 10 KPH
- **LIKES:** TRACKING ANIMALS AND EXPLORING WILDLIFE
- **DISLIKES:** RAINY DAYS

Tom's eye   Tom's hand

WANNA

- **FULL NAME:** WANNANOSAURUS
- **AGE:** 65 – 80 MILLION YEARS**
- **SIZE:** LESS THAN A JATOM*
- **TOP SPEED:** 50 KPH, ESPECIALLY WHEN BEING CHASED BY A T-REX
- **LIKES:** STINKY GINGKO FRUIT AND BANGING HIS HEAD ON TREE TRUNKS
- **DISLIKES:** SCARY DINOSAURS

Wanna's head   Wanna's foot

*NOTE: A JATOM IS THE SIZE OF JAMIE OR TOM: 125 CM TALL AND 27 KG IN WEIGHT
**NOTE: SCIENTISTS CALL THIS PERIOD THE LATE CRETACEOUS

DIPLODOCUS

Diplodocus's eye

Diplodocus's teeth

Diplodocus's foot

Diplodocus's tail

- **FULL NAME:** DIPLODOCUS
- **LENGTH:** 20 JATOMS*
- **WEIGHT:** 400 JATOMS*
- **AGE:** ABOUT 150 MILLION YEARS***
- **HEIGHT:** (HEAD DOWN): 4 JATOMS*
- **HEIGHT:** (HEAD UP): 11 JATOMS*
- **LIKES:** NIBBLING THE TOPS OF TREES AND WHIPPING ITS TAIL
- **DISLIKES:** SPLINTERS AND TOOTHACHES

* **NOTE:** A JATOM IS THE SIZE OF JAMIE OR TOM: 125 CM TALL AND 27 KG IN WEIGHT
*** **NOTE:** SCIENTISTS CALL THIS PERIOD THE JURASSIC

DINOSAUR COVE

Village

Marina

SealighT Head

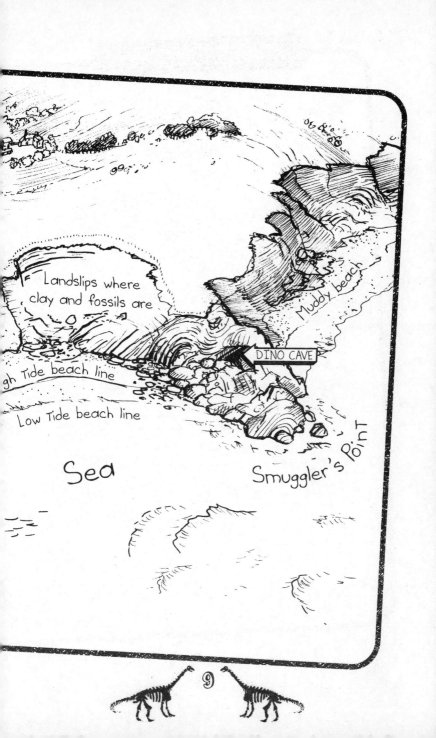

Landslips where
clay and fossils are

DINO CAVE

Muddy beach

gh Tide beach line

Low Tide beach line

Sea

Smuggler's Point

'Where are you, Grandad?' Jamie Morgan's voice echoed round the dinosaur museum on the ground floor of the lighthouse. 'We're off to hunt for dinosaurs!'

'He'll think we mean fossil dinosaurs, not real ones,' Tom Clay whispered. The two friends grinned at one another. Only they knew the amazing secret of Dinosaur Cove— a cave that led to a world of real live dinosaurs!

'Grandad?' Jamie called again. As he slung his backpack over his shoulders and stepped

into the lobby of the museum, his feet
scrunched on something gritty.

'Why are these seeds all over the floor?'
Tom wondered. 'Maybe he's gardening?'

They hurried out of the front door and
looked around the cliff top. There was no
sign of Grandad.

There was a flash of yellow as a little bird
with a red head swooped down and began to
peck at something on a flat rock beside a
bush near the edge of the cliff.

'Look,' Tom said, pointing to the trail of
seeds that led to the rock where the bird was
feasting. The branches of the bush rustled.

'Grandad?' Jamie called, making the
bird fly off.

'Shhhhh!' hissed the bush.

Jamie laughed in surprise as
Grandad's mop of unruly hair
emerged from the leaves.

'What are you doing in a bush?' Jamie asked, running over.

'This is my bird hide,' Grandad whispered. 'I'm taking part in a survey, recording all the different birds that visit Dinosaur Cove. That was a goldfinch.'

shhhhh!

'Sorry, we scared it away,' Tom said.

'It'll come back to the birdseed.' The captain's eyes twinkled. 'It can't resist the bait. Why don't you boys try a spot of bird watching?'

'Awesome idea! We know just the place to do it.' Jamie nudged Tom.

Grandad held up his finger. 'Remember, the secret of bird watching is stay quiet and hidden.' He tapped his nose, then ducked back into the bush.

'See you later, Grandad!' Jamie called.

They raced off along the path towards Smuggler's Point.

'Got the ammonite?' Tom asked.

Jamie patted his pocket. 'The Jurassic one,' he confirmed as they reached the cave. The spiral fossil was the key to which time period they would visit.

Jamie took out his torch and they squeezed through the tiny gap at the back of the cave into the secret chamber that led to Dino World. His heart was thumping with excitement as he fitted his feet into the fossil footprints. He took a deep breath and stepped towards the cave wall. 'One, two, three, four . . . FIVE!'

A crack of light appeared in the solid rock and suddenly he was in the sweltering sunlight of Dino World. His ears filled with the sounds of insects buzzing and the strange calls of unseen creatures out there in the Jurassic jungle.

There was a squelch as Tom trod on the slimy leaf mould beside him, stirring up a familiar smell in the hot humid air.

'Phew!' Tom gagged. 'The gingko fruit must be ripe. They're even stinkier than usual.'

'Wanna will love them.' Jamie pulled a face.

At the mention of his name, a little dinosaur with a bony head bounded up to the boys on his two back legs, wagging his tail and making happy grunking noises.

'He's pleased to see us.' Tom laughed. 'It's good to see you again, Wanna.'

Wanna looked up hopefully at the fruit-laden gingko tree.

'I'll get you one.' Jamie wrinkled his nose and reached out for an apricot-sized fruit on a nearby branch. It was so ripe that sticky gingko goo squished through his fingers.

He tried to toss the fruit to the little dinosaur
but it stuck fast to his hand.

'Yuck!' Jamie held out his hand. Wanna
slurped down the fruit, then licked the
sticky juice off Jamie's fingers with his
sandpaper tongue.

'Gross!' Jamie wiped off the
dino drool on to
his jeans.

'Since Wanna's
so mad about
gingkoes,'
Tom said
thoughtfully,
'maybe we
should take some
along to bait flying
reptiles, like birdseed.'

'We'll be the very first
Jurassic birdwatchers.'

Jamie filled a plastic bag
with the foul-smelling fruit and
stuffed it in his backpack. He held
out his hands for Wanna to clean.

'Let's go dino bird watching!'

CHAPTER 2

SEARCH:

G H I J K L M N
. . . . . Y Z ENTER

Tom and Jamie plunged into the steamy
Jurassic jungle, and began to wade through
the sea of ferns beneath the tall conifer trees.
Wanna followed them closely, with his eyes
firmly fixed on Jamie's backpack.

Tom looked up.

'What is it?' Jamie asked, pushing a fern
out of his face.

'I can't see anything,' Tom complained as
another fern twanged to and fro in front of his
face. 'We need to find a gap in the jungle.'

They pressed on through the thick
undergrowth until they came to a clearing
scattered with enormous flat rocks.

'This looks like a good place for bird
watching,' Tom said. 'Where shall we hide?'

Jamie looked round. 'How about up
there?' He pointed to a tall tree on the
edge of the clearing. It was draped with
thick rope-like vines. Halfway up, two
sturdy branches emerged from the
trunk together, making a safe platform
to sit on.

'Looks good,' Tom agreed, 'but the
birds might see us.'

'Not if we make a dino-bird hide!' Jamie said excitedly.

'Cool,' Tom grinned. 'Like a tree house.'

'We can use ferns for the roof and sides . . .' Jamie grabbed hold of the thick stem of a broad leaf fern and pulled with all his might. 'I can't pull it up,' he panted, 'it's too tough.'

As he spoke, the fern gave way with a sudden pop and he fell backwards into the soggy leaf mould. He stood up covered in mud, with pine needles and bits of dead fern sticking all over him.

'I look like a swamp monster,' he spluttered.

Tom laughed. 'But it's awesome
camouflage. A bit more and you'll look like
part of the jungle.' He grabbed a handful of
tender fern tips and stuffed them down the
neck of Jamie's T-shirt.

'I'll get you for that!' Jamie scooped up an
armful of soft mud and leaf mould and hurled
it towards Tom.

Tom stepped sideways and the muck hit
Wanna. *Splat!*

'Missed me!' Tom burst into laughter at
the sight of the muck-covered dinosaur.
Wanna didn't seem to like that. He wagged
his tail and lowered his head.

'Go, Wanna, go!' Jamie cheered as Wanna gently barged Tom into the muddy ooze. Jamie rushed over and stuffed some fern tips down his friend's neck.

'Now you're camouflaged too!' Jamie bent double laughing.

After a moment, Tom struggled to his feet. 'We'll scare away the wildlife with all this noise. Let's get on with making the hide.'

The boys both gathered an armful of dead leaves, then climbed the tree and began weaving them through the dangling vines to make the sides of the hide.

Down below, Wanna put his head on one side and watched curiously. Then he sighed deeply and curled up in the ferns.

'Wanna's taking a nap,' Jamie whispered, peering down at the little dinosaur through a gap in the fern wall.

'That's good,' Tom said, laying the last of the ferns across the top of the hide to make a roof. 'Let's hope he stays still and quiet.'

Jamie took out his notebook and wrote DINO BIRD SURVEY at the top of one page. Tom smiled, then they peered out through the fern wall into the clearing, watching and waiting.

After a few minutes, something flapped onto the branch of the tree above them.

Through a gap in the fern roof, Jamie could see the claws on the creature's feet gripping on to the branch. It looked like an overgrown woodpecker with electric blue feathers. 'Archaeopteryx,' he breathed.

'Awesome,' Tom whispered. 'Its beak's full of razor-sharp teeth.'

As Jamie leaned closer, the fern tips sticking out of his T-shirt tickled his nose. 'A . . . a . . . atishoo!' he sneezed.

The archaeopteryx took off in an explosion of twigs. Something white and

slimy splattered on the fern roof of the
hide and dripped down, narrowly missing
Jamie's shoulder.

'Yurgh!' Tom grimaced.

'...Archaeopteryx poo!'

Jamie smiled and opened his notebook
to the dino bird survey page. He wrote
'Archaeopteryx 1' and sketched a picture of
the bird. They had seen an archaeopteryx on
an earlier adventure in Dino World. Jamie
hoped the next entry would be something new
and even more exciting.

'Let's put out some gingkoes,' Tom whispered, taking the plastic bag out of Jamie's backpack.

'Don't wake Wanna,' Jamie warned him. 'Or he'll eat them all.'

As quietly as he could, Tom stretched up his arm and squished a gingko fruit onto a branch, sticking it down.

'Let's see what takes the bait,' he whispered.

The boys sat peering through the gaps in the ferns, waiting for the dino birds.

Nothing came. Jamie shifted uncomfortably on the branch. It was hard sitting still and waiting, but the boys were determined. Tom flipped open the Fossil Finder to pass the time. He tapped in *JURASSIC FLYING REPTILES*. 'My favourite flier's

DIMORPHODON

SEARCH: JURASSIC FLYING REPTILES

the dimorphodon,' he told Jamie. 'It has a beak like a puffin.'

'Shh,' Jamie whispered.

Just then, the branches of the conifer rustled as a dark orange pterosaur with a wingspan as wide as Jamie's outstretched arms landed on the branch.

'Is it a dimorphodon?' Tom asked.

The creature scooped up a jawful of gingko fruit, dangling its long thin tail with a kite-shaped tip in front of their noses.

'No, that's a rhamphorhynchus,' Jamie whispered excitedly, noting it down on his dino bird survey.

Tom looked closely at the flying reptile's long, thin jaws. 'Its teeth criss-cross,' he said in surprise.

30

Jamie started to sketch the creature.
Thunk!

The tree trunk wobbled and Jamie only
just managed to hang on to his notebook.
Beneath them, Wanna was standing back
from the tree. He lowered his head and
barged it into the trunk.

Thunk! The tree wobbled again. The
rhamphorhynchus launched itself into the air
with a squawk.

'Stop it, Wanna!' Tom called down. 'You'll scare everything away.'

'He must be bored,' Jamie said. 'A few gingkoes will keep him quiet.' He dropped a stinky fruit, which splattered at Wanna's feet. But the little dinosaur took no notice. He head-butted the tree again.

Thunk!

Tom and Jamie looked at each other.

'I don't believe it,' Jamie gasped. 'Wanna *never* ignores gingkoes.'

'Something's wrong,' Tom said nervously.

The tree shook.

'That wasn't Wanna,' Tom gulped. 'Wanna's trying to warn us. Something's coming!'

CHAPTER 3

A humongous dappled-green lizardy head
burst through the front wall of their fern hide,
tearing it clean away.

'Get down!' Jamie shouted as the creature
swept off the flimsy roof and opened its
toothy jaws.

The boys flattened themselves against the
thick branch they were sitting on.

Scruuuuunch!

The tree shook as the long-necked dinosaur
stripped the vines from the branch above them.

Tom gulped. 'What is it?'

The gigantic beast grabbed hold of another branch and raked off the pine needles, chewing the greenery with its peg-like teeth.

Jamie heaved a huge sigh of relief. 'It's a plant eater.'

Tom grinned. 'And with those nostrils on the top of its snout, it's got to be a diplodocus!' Jamie pulled out his Fossil

Finder and looked up diplodocus.

'IT EATS TONS OF VEGETATION A DAY TO FUEL ITS HUGE BODY, BUT DOESN'T STOP TO CHEW,' he read. 'IT SWALLOWS STONES TO GRIND UP ITS FOOD.'

'Cool,' Tom said. 'It's an eating machine.'

Jamie stashed the Fossil Finder and his notebook in his backpack as the diplodocus's nose swept away the rest of the fern hide. It sniffed deeply and moved towards Jamie. Its long neck and head were covered in giraffe-like markings in shades of jungle green.

'Keep still,' Tom hissed. 'It wants to eat your ferns, not you!'

The dinosaur's rubbery lips nuzzled at the fresh fern tips sticking out of the neck of Jamie's T-shirt.

'It tickles!' Jamie giggled as the lizardy lips nibbled at the leaves. Below them, Wanna had settled down, realizing that they weren't in danger.

Tom pulled the fern leaves out of his shirt and held them out on the palm of his hand. 'Here you are.'

The gigantic beast took them gently and gulped them down.

'It's like feeding a huge horse,' Tom whispered.

The boys watched as the diplodocus stripped more branches of pine needles and

swallowed some of the smaller twigs
whole, leaving bare branches draped
with dinosaur drool.

'This tree would make better dino
toothpicks than lunch,' Jamie commented.

'There are some younger creepers and
branches at the top, Dippy,' Tom
said. 'Those would be tastier.'

As if it'd heard, the huge dino
reared up on its hind legs.

'Awesome!' Jamie murmured.
They could see the diplodocus's
pale yellow tummy as its
elephantine front legs pawed
the air and it stretched out
its long neck to grab the
thickest branch at the
top of the tree.

The branch bent,
but instead of raking off

the leaves and the creepers, the dinosaur hung on to it. The whole tree began to bend and shake.

'Dippy! Let go of the branch,' Tom shouted, hugging the shuddering tree.

There was a *craaack* as the branch broke off and a thump as the diplodocus's feet hit the earth. The tree swayed back and forth, but the boys managed to cling to their branch.

'Phew!' Jamie breathed. Beneath them, they could see Dippy

contentedly champing at the branch,
breaking it into small pieces to gulp down.
Suddenly, the dinosaur's eyes bulged and
it swung its head up and began to shake it
violently from side to side, making frantic
sucking sounds with
its tongue.

'What's happening now?' Tom looked
worried.

'I'm not sure,' Jamie replied, 'but it doesn't
look good.'

The dinosaur's movements became even
more erratic and the boys worried about
Wanna getting trampled on the ground.

'Dippy's freaking out!' Tom yelled.
'Let's get out of here before it knocks us off.'

But before they could scramble down the
tree, Dippy started to bellow, rearing up on its
hind legs and thrashing its front feet.

'Hang on,' Jamie yelled as two huge
dinosaur feet flailed at the tree.

The tree bent and sprang back, catapulting
Tom off the branch. Jamie watched helplessly

as his friend fell, clawing wildly at the air.
Luckily, he landed on the diplodocus's neck,
wrapping his arms around it to stop himself
falling further.

'I meant hang on to the tree, not
the dinosaur!' Jamie yelled as
the huge dinosaur stomped into the jungle
with Tom swinging from its long, swaying
neck.

CHAPTER 4

From his tree, Jamie could see Dippy shaking
its head wildly from side to side. Any minute
now, Tom would fall off or be crushed against
a tree trunk. He had to save his friend!

The end of a thick creeper dangled before
him. Jamie took a deep breath, grabbed on to
the vine and launched himself towards the
next tree. He swung safely across to a thick
branch with more vines hanging down. He
took hold and leapt off, swinging from tree to
tree through the jungle after Tom.

Beneath him,
Wanna was leaping
logs and dodging
branches in his
struggle to keep up.
'Yee-haw!'
Jamie called as he
swung, and soon he
was alongside the
lumbering diplodocus.
Tom had slipped
round the underside

of the dinosaur's
neck, just below
its head, and was
clinging on for dear
life.

'Help!' Tom
shouted at the top
of his lungs. 'I
can't hold on
much longer!'

'I'll get you,'
Jamie shouted back.
He launched himself onto another
vine and swung across Dippy's path.
'Grab my hand!'

The boys' fingertips brushed as
Jamie swung past the dinosaur's eyes,
but he wasn't close enough to reach Tom.

Dippy stopped thrashing its head and
looked in amazement as Jamie swung back on
to the tree.

'I'm coming again.' Jamie took a deep breath and launched himself from the same vine. He swung towards Tom, rising higher and higher, right above the dino's head! At the top of the swing, he stretched his hand down to Tom. Tom reached up, and they interlocked their fingers.

Jamie had him!

Snap! The vine gave way.

Jamie plummeted down, and was only saved by his friend's firm grip. While Tom held on to Dippy's neck with all his might, Jamie pulled himself up towards the giant reptile's scaly head and clawed for a handhold. He grabbed what felt like a slimy rubbery ledge. He was dangling from Dippy's spitty bottom lip.

Whoooooooo!

Dippy dropped its head and Jamie quickly let go and tumbled to the ground. Tom landed in a heap beside him.

As Dippy pulled away, Jamie could see a piece of wood the size of a baseball bat lodged between the dinosaur's brown teeth and rubbery green gums.

'That was awesome!' Tom gasped. 'I've never swung from a dinosaur before.'

'First time for me, too,' Jamie panted, trying to catch his breath as he untangled himself from his backpack.

Wanna hurtled out of the jungle and leapt on them, grunking enthusiastically.

'Gerroff, we're ok!' Jamie struggled to

grunk!

grunk

grunk

his feet.

Whoooooo!

Dippy was wailing again, scraping its jaws along the ground. Then it lifted its head and shook it from side to side.

'I know what's making it so crazy,' Jamie told Tom. 'I saw a splinter of branch stuck between its teeth.'

As they watched the huge dinosaur stomp off again, Tom said, 'Poor Dippy's got a toothache.'

Jamie nodded. 'I had toothache once and it really hurt.'

'We need a dinosaur dentist,' Tom said, 'but we can't just call one up.'

The boys looked at each other and grinned.

'Let's go after it,' Jamie said.

Tom nodded. 'We'll be Dippy's dentists!'

'Follow Dippy!' Tom set off in the direction of a series of circular dents in the leaf mould on the jungle floor.

Wanna dashed ahead and stopped at a mound of slimy orange mush, bobbing his head up and down.

'Good thing Dippy's left a clear trail,' Jamie commented.

'He's squashed ferns too,' Tom pointed out a heap of crushed fronds.

Something wet and slimy splattered down Jamie's neck. Slimy strings of frothy saliva were dripping from the tree Dippy had been walking under.

'Dino drool,' he told Tom. 'Dippy must have scraped its mouth against the branch to try and get that splinter out of its jaw.'

The trail led them to a part of the jungle criss-crossed with pathways and dinosaur footprints.

'Other diplodocus are using these paths,' Jamie said in dismay. 'I can't make out Dippy's trail.'

The boys scanned the jungle.

'I think it went this way.' Tom set off along a well-trodden jungle path, but Wanna grabbed his sleeve and dug his heels into the ground.

Jamie laughed. 'I think Wanna thinks you're going the wrong way.'

Wanna let go of Tom and then set off at a brisk trot down another pathway.

The boys chased after Wanna and soon burst into a clearing scattered with enormous flat rocks.

'We're back where we started!' Jamie exclaimed. 'We've gone round in a circle.'

'There's Dippy.' Tom pointed to the far side of the rocks. 'It looks exhausted.'

The huge dinosaur was dragging its enormous feet and staggering. As they watched, Dippy's legs buckled and it fell with a humongous

CRASH!

The earth shuddered beneath Tom's and Jamie's feet and there was a moment's silence in the jungle before the insects resumed their relentless buzzing.

Dippy lay on its side, with its long neck and tail stretched out.

'Oh no,' Jamie said. 'Is it dead?'

'No,' Tom replied. 'Its rib cage is moving and there's froth

bubbling from its mouth. It's just exhausted.
We can still help.'

They hurried towards the collapsed
dinosaur. Its beady eyes looked at them, but it
didn't move. Oily tears oozed from Dippy's
eyes. It opened its mouth with a pitiful low.
Whooooooooo.

'We've got to get that splinter out,' Tom said. 'If it's too exhausted to move, the Jurassic scavengers will get it.'

'A real dentist would get it out in no time,' Jamie said.

'It'd never fit in a dentist's chair!' Tom joked.

Jamie and Tom lay on their tummies and wriggled up to the dinosaur's mouth. A blast of warm dino breath and frothy saliva hit them full in the face.

'Yuck!' Jamie gagged. 'Its breath smells like rotten eggs.'

'I can't see the splinter,' Tom said, wiping the froth away from Dippy's jaws. 'We need to get rid of some of this spit.'

Jamie helped and soon the boys could see Dippy's teeth, like two rows of brown tent pegs set in rubbery green gums. The splinter was stuck in its gum between two back teeth.

'I think I can get it out.' Jamie gently reached his arm inside the dinosaur's mouth and grabbed the end of the splinter. The Dippy's mouth felt warm and slimy.

Whoooooooooo.

The gigantic beast moaned but kept still.

'Careful,' Tom breathed.

'Open wide, Dippy.' Jamie tugged at the splinter, but his hands only slipped down the wood.

'Do real dentists get covered in this much spit?' Jamie groaned. 'I can't get a good grip.'

'Let me try,' Tom told him.

Jamie wriggled to one side and wiped the dino drool on his jeans while Tom reached in.

'It's much too slimy,' Tom agreed.

Dippy closed his eyes as the boys sat back on their heels.

'We're not helping; we're just hurting it more,' Tom said with a frown.

Above them came the sound of flapping wings. Dark grey shapes began to circle like vultures above the exhausted diplodocus.

'Pterodactyls.' Jamie leapt to his feet and shook his fists at them. 'Go away!' he yelled.

Wanna took one look at them and dashed into the jungle.

The sharp-beaked pterodactyls flapped
onto the branch of a nearby tree and sat
there, hunched and waiting.

CHAPTER 6

Wanna crept back into the clearing with a mouthful of soft juicy ferns, and put them straight into Dippy's mouth.

Dippy half-heartedly spat them out.

'It's a good idea to feed it.' Tom patted Wanna's head. 'But it's in too much pain to eat.'

'It'll die if we give up on it,' Jamie said, glancing up at the pterodactyls. 'We have to keep trying. How can we get a better grip on that splinter?'

Wanna began hopping from foot to foot, grunking hopefully.

'He wants a gingko,' Tom said. 'You'd better give him one or he'll never let us get on with it.'

Jamie got out the plastic bag. All the remaining gingko fruit were squashed together in a stinky sticky mess.

'Yuck!' He opened the bag and lay it on the ground in front of Wanna. Wanna sniffed at the bag but didn't make a move to eat the gingkoes; he just looked at Jamie, panting.

Jamie tried to wipe off the foul smelling juice on his T-shirt, but it was stuck fast to his hands.

'That's what Wanna was trying to tell us,' Jamie said. 'We can use gingko glue!' He took another handful of mushy gingkoes out of the bag and wriggled on his tummy up to Dippy's jaws.

Tom grabbed a handful of gingko pulp as well and crawled over to help.

Jamie gently mashed the gooey gingkoes along the splinter of wood. 'It's sticking!'

Tom knelt beside Jamie. 'I'll grab on too.'

Together they started pulling. 'It's moving,' Jamie said. There was a sucking, squelching sound then the boys fell backwards as the splinter came free.

Whooo!

Dippy seemed relieved.

The splinter was as long as Jamie's arm with a sharp point, covered in mucus. Jamie tossed it into the undergrowth and then watched as Wanna nudged the soft ferns towards the huge dinosaur. Dippy gulped them down and raised its head.

Sluuurp! Sluurp! Sluurp!

A wet tongue the size of a bath towel, covered in spitty bits of fern and gingko goo, licked each of them in turn.

Sluuurp! Sluurp!

Sluuurp!

'He's going to be OK.' Jamie and Tom leaped to their feet and shouted out in celebration. The vulture-like pterodactyls in the tree took off in alarm.

Dippy slowly clambered to its feet. Then it gently lowered its head and nuzzled first the boys, then Wanna, before turning and lumbering off into the forest.

'We did it!' Jamie grinned, wiping diplodocus drool off his face with the back of his hand. 'We are dino dentists!'

They gave each other a high five. Gingko goop spattered down their bare arms.

'Help, Wanna!' Jamie and Tom shouted together, holding out their arms. They cringed as Wanna's sandpapery tongue rasped off every trace of gingko juice.

'It's probably time to go,' Jamie said.

'But we haven't seen a dimorphodon,' Tom said.

'We've used all the gingkoes,' Jamie reminded him, 'so we can't bait any more birds.'

'I suppose we've done enough "bird" watching for one day,' Tom agreed as they set off for Gingko Cave. 'Archaeopteryx, rhamphorhynchus, and those horrible pterodactyls.'

As they came to the clearing in front of the shallow cave, Jamie put his arm out to stop Tom. He put his finger to his lips.

'Look,' he whispered. The ground was splattered with slimy ripe gingkoes. Waddling among them was a sand-coloured creature, the size of a cat, with leathery wings and a long spiky tail.

The boys watched as it sank its big red beak into the stinky fruit.

'Dimorphodon.' Tom whispered. 'My favourite flier.'

The boys watched it for a moment until Wanna hurtled out of the jungle and the dimorphodon took off, flapping away over the tree tops, honking as it flew. Wanna skidded to a halt and started to slurp up the gingkoes.

Jamie smiled. 'Wanna is rubbish at bird watching.'

'He likes the bait too much,' Tom replied. 'See you next time, Wanna!'

The little dinosaur lifted his snout from
the gingkoes and wagged his tail as the boys
stepped backwards into the footprints.
The ground turned to stone beneath their
feet and once more they were back in
the secret chamber at the back of
the smugglers' cave.

'Dino dentistry has made me hungry,' Jamie said, as they dashed to the lighthouse.

'Grandad!' he called from the lighthouse door. 'We're back! We're so hungry we could eat a dinosaur.'

'Up here, me hearties,' came the answering cry. The boys raced up the stairs to the kitchen.

Owwwww!

'I'll make some of my famous cheese and pickle sandwiches,' the captain told them with a grin. 'They'll only take a couple of minutes.'

'I can't wait that long.' Jamie spotted his grandad's jar of boiled sweets. He grabbed one and bit into it.

'Owwwww! My tooth!' he yelled.

'You're making more noise than a dinosaur at the dentist,' Tom told him.

Jamie spluttered. 'Not as much noise as someone swinging from the neck of a diplodocus.'

'I wish I had your imaginations.' Grandad laughed as he cut up the sandwiches. 'You sound as if you've had a fun day.'

Jamie and Tom grinned at each other.

'We always have fun in Dinosaur Cove!'

DINOSAUR WORLD

BOYS' ROUTE

Humongous Waterfall

Massive Canyon

Plains

Fin Rock

Jurassic Ocean

Misty Mountains

Thick Jungle

Gingko Cave

Discovery Hills

GLOSSARY

Ammonite (am-on-ite) – an extinct animal with octopus-like legs and often a spiral-shaped shell that lived in the ocean.

Archaeopteryx (ar-kee-op-ter-ix) – the earliest bird capable of flight, with sharp teeth, three clawed fingers, and a long bony tail. Archaeopteryx was not a fussy feeder, eating small animals, plants, and insects.

Dimorphodon (di-mor-foh-don) – a flying reptile that had a long, pointed tail and big head with two different types of teeth.

Diplodocus (dip-lod-oh-kus) – one of the longest land dinosaurs with a long neck and whip-like tail. This huge dinosaur had pencil-shaped blunt teeth perfect for its plant-only diet.

Gingko (gink-oh) – a tree native to China called a 'living fossil' because fossils of it have been found dating back millions of years, yet they are still around today. Also known as the stink bomb tree because of its smelly apricot-like fruit.

Jurassic – from about 150 to 200 million years ago, the Jurassic age was warm and humid, with lush jungle cover and great marine diversity. Large dinosaurs ruled on land, while the first birds took to the air.

Pterodactyl (ter-oh-dak-til) – a flying prehistoric reptile which could be as small as a bird or as large as an aeroplane.

Pterosaur (ter-oh-sor) – a prehistoric flying reptile. Its wings were leathery and light and some of these 'winged lizards' had fur on their bodies and bony crests on their heads.

Rhamphorhynchus (ram-foh-ring-kus) – meat-eating flying reptile with a diamond-shaped point of skin at the end of its long tail.

Wannanosaurus (wah-nan-oh-sor-us) – a dinosaur that only ate plants and used its hard, flat skull to defend itself. Named after the place it was discovered: Wannano in China.

You'd better start running
... I'm coming after you!